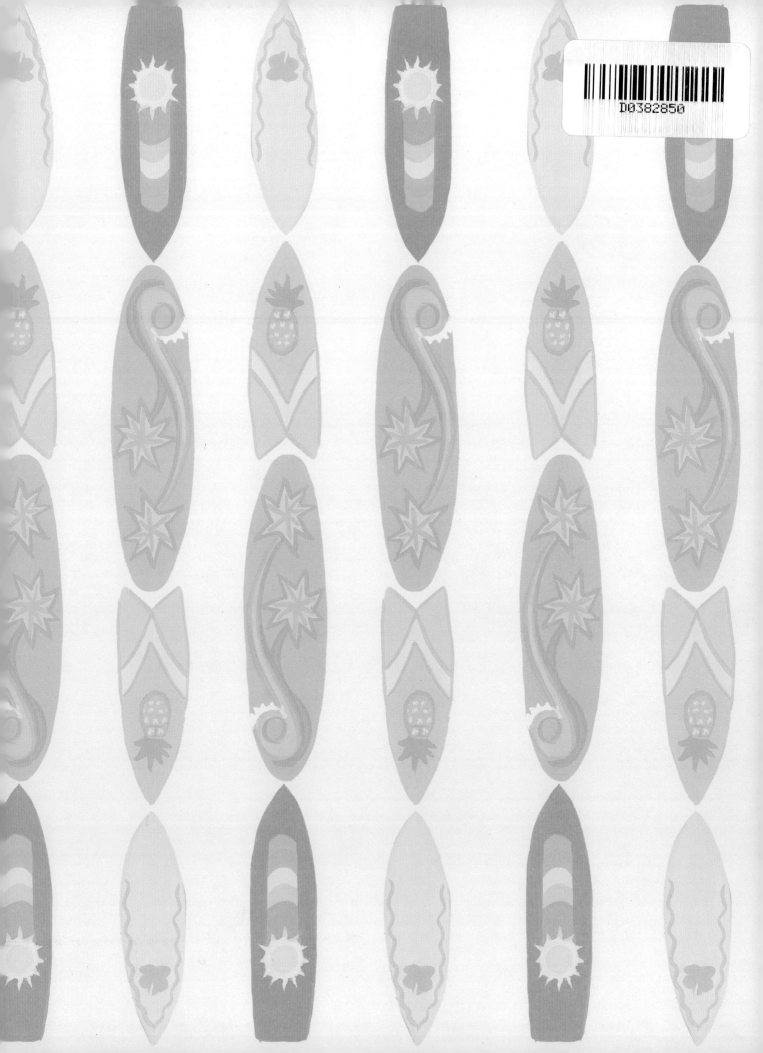

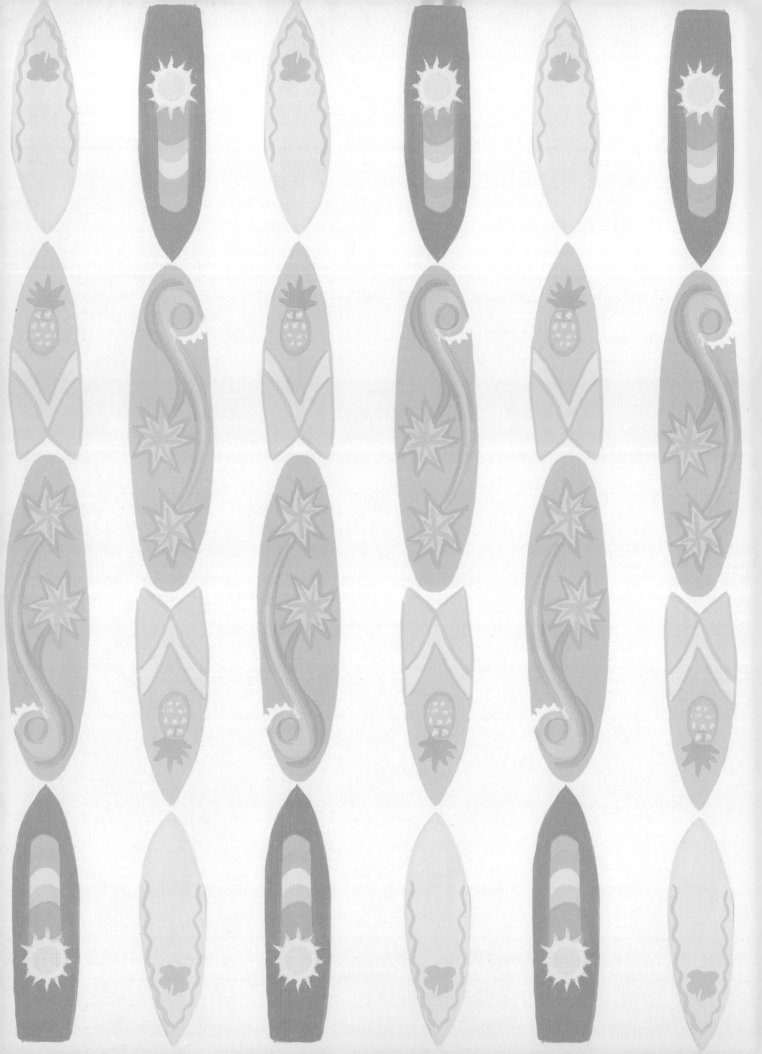

A Story of Surfing

Written and Illustrated by

Carla Golembe

3565 Harding Avenue
Honolulu, Hawai'i 96816
phone: (808) 734-7159
fax: (808) 732-3627
e-mail: sales@besspress.com
http://www.besspress.com

Hawaiian words:

ali'i	chiefs, royalty
aloha	hello, goodbye, love, and spirit that comes from the heart
hau	tree with light wood once used to make canoe outriggers
hōpūpū	excited, stoked
'ohana	family
olo	long surfboard made of *wiliwili* or *koa* wood
wāhine	women
wiliwili	native Hawaiian tree; its seeds are used in *lei* and its light wood was once used to make surfboards, canoe outriggers, and floats for nets.

Surf lingo:

break	area in the water where the waves break
crest	top of the wave
paddle out	lie on the board and use your arms to move yourself and the board out to the break
pop up	stand up on the surfboard in almost one motion
set	group of waves
stoked	excited about going surfing; full of energy
watermen	(and waterwomen) surfers, swimmers, sailors, and others who work and play in the water
wave sliding	*he'e nalu*, the ancient Hawaiian term for surfing
wipe out	fall off the surfboard

Who's who:

Duke Kahanamoku (1890-1968) Hawaiian surfer, swimmer, and all-around waterman known as the International Father of Modern Surfing and Hawai'i's Ambassador of Aloha

Hau Tree Boys group of young surfers who gathered beneath a *hau* tree on Waikīkī Beach in the early 1900s. Some of these "beach boys" later formed the famous Hui Nalu surf club.

Mary Ann Hawkins (1919-1993) champion swimmer, surfer, body surfer, and paddle boarder considered by many to be the best female surfer of the first half of the twentieth century

Māmala Hawaiian chiefess celebrated in legend as the earliest known female surfer. It was said she could take the form of a shark.

Rell Sunn (1950-1998) champion surfer and all-around waterwoman who was Hawai'i's first full-time female lifeguard and an organizer of the Women's Professional Surfing Association

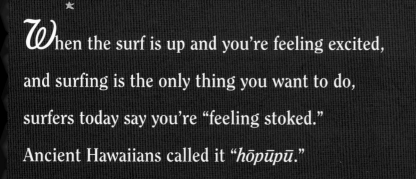

When the surf is up and you're feeling excited,
and surfing is the only thing you want to do,
surfers today say you're "feeling stoked."
Ancient Hawaiians called it "*hōpūpū*."

Three or four thousand years ago,
Polynesians first stood on boards on the sea.
They brought wave sliding to our shores
when they came in canoes to Hawai'i.

Keana loved to swim and dive.

She loved all things about the sea.

She liked to watch her uncle surf

Out on the breaks at Waikīkī.

It looked so magical to her.

"Please, Uncle, teach me to surf!" she cried.

"Be patient, Keana, I'll teach you soon,

when you're strong and older," he replied.

Keana wondered, When is soon?

And then, one day when she was eight,

Uncle asked, "Are you ready?"

"Oh yes!"

"Tomorrow, then, we have a date.

"Are you ready to fly along the sea?

Are you ready to glide along the waves?

It's the very best feeling in the world.

To do it, though, you must be brave."

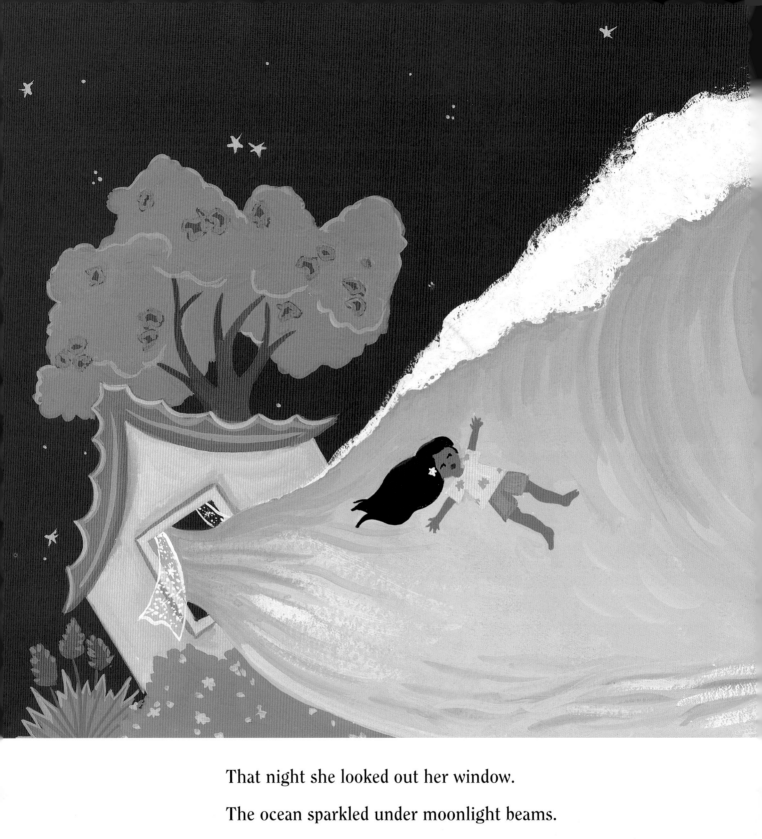

That night she looked out her window.

The ocean sparkled under moonlight beams.

She watched the glow upon the sea

and fell into the land of dreams.

In her dream the ocean picked her up

and carried her gently to a shore

where vines and palm trees grew untamed

and she saw no houses, cars, or stores,

No streetlights, only the sounds of waves.
There, by a surfboard, stood a boy.
"*Aloha*," he said and nodded his head
and greeted her with a smile of joy.

"Who are you?" Keana asked.
"And tell me, what is this land so wild?"
"You're in Hawai'i of long ago,
and I'm Keo, the prince, an *ali'i* child."

Keana pointed. "What is that?"
"My *olo* board, of *wiliwili* wood.
It's really long and weighs a lot.
It's the board of chiefs—it's very good.

"We *ali'i* have our private beaches.
Each one is a special place
where we hold our competitions
to show our courage, strength, and grace.

"Before he makes a board, the shaper
turns and faces toward the sea
and gives thanks for the wood he'll use
by burying a fish beneath the tree."

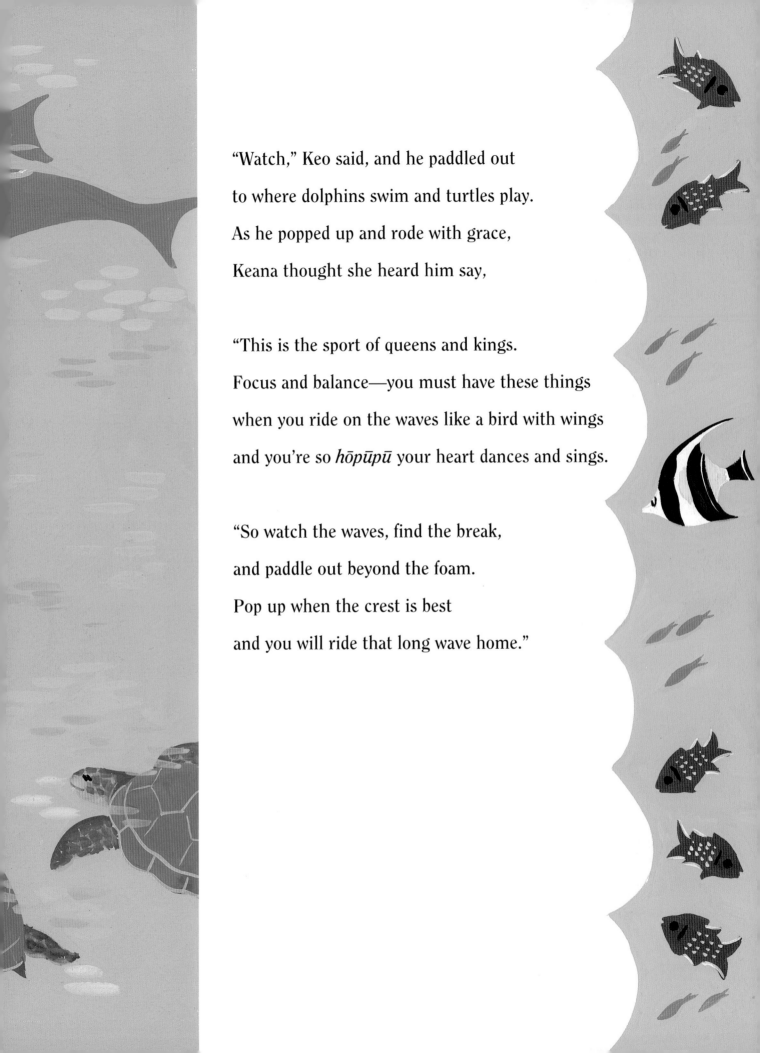

"Watch," Keo said, and he paddled out
to where dolphins swim and turtles play.
As he popped up and rode with grace,
Keana thought she heard him say,

"This is the sport of queens and kings.
Focus and balance—you must have these things
when you ride on the waves like a bird with wings
and you're so *hōpūpū* your heart dances and sings.

"So watch the waves, find the break,
and paddle out beyond the foam.
Pop up when the crest is best
and you will ride that long wave home."

Then that wave picked Keana up.

To the top of the stars she seemed to climb.

When it washed her onto the sandy shore,

she found herself in a different time.

She was on the beach at Waikīkī

at the start of the twentieth century.

She looked around and saw some surfers
gathered beneath an old *hau* tree.

"*Aloha*," one said. "My name is Duke,
and we're known as the Hau Tree Boys.
Beneath this tree we've formed a club
to bring back surfing's skills and joys."

"Bring back?" Keana asked them all. "What's happened to the royal sport?"

"Come sit with us," Duke said to her. "We'll give you the complete report.

"There was a time when people came here from distant foreign lands.

They didn't feel connected to the ocean, surf, and sand.

"'Surfing is lazy, sinful, bad! Get to work,' they cried.

The Hawaiians listened to their words, and surfing almost died.

"But we're reviving surfing now. Our clubs have meets and competitions.

We're showing surfing to the world and riding the waves in new positions.

"Soon surfing will spread all over the world. Light fiberglass boards will be the fashion.

But always the key to a surfer's heart is to catch and ride the waves with passion.

"We watch the waves, find the break, and paddle out beyond the foam.

We pop up when the crest is best, and then we ride those big waves home."

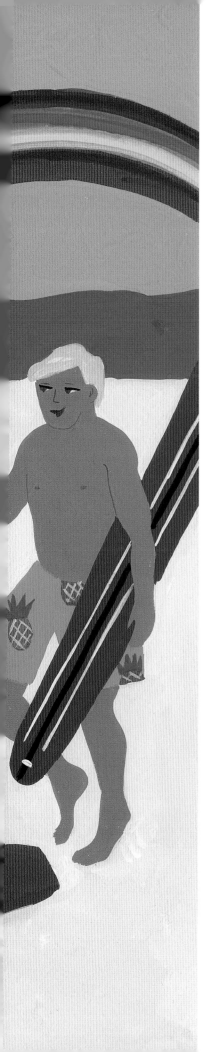

Keana rose up on the waves.
They carried her away,
Along O'ahu's wild North Shore
to the edge of Waimea Bay.

Some young men hung out on the beach,
their faces toward the sun.
Their pants were baggy, their hair was shaggy,
and they were having fun.

"We've come from California
to face these waves, their splendid danger.
We live near the beach and surf all day,
and no one among us is a stranger.

"Waimea has the biggest waves.
It's a surfer's paradise—it's heaven.
We're going to make history,
Now, in nineteen fifty-seven.

"No one has ridden waves this big—
twenty, thirty, forty feet tall.
The ocean reaches to the sky,
a giant, swirling, foaming wall.

"You can watch us, but you can't surf here.
Your first rides must be gentle.
Get to know the ocean first
and learn the surfing fundamentals."

Keana watched the watermen,
she listened to the ocean roar,
and as she saw them catching waves,
They called out to her on the shore.

"Watch the waves, find the break,
and paddle out beyond the foam.
Pop up when the crest is best
and ride that giant all the way home."

Once more the ocean picked her up
and placed her on glistening sands.
Three women stood in front of her.
They smiled, and each held out her hands.

"Welcome, Keana, my name is Rell.
This is Māmala and here's Mary Ann.
We wanted to make sure you knew
not every surfer is a man.

"There have always been *wāhine* surfers,
waterwomen strong and smart.
And when you paddle out tomorrow,
keep us with you in your heart."

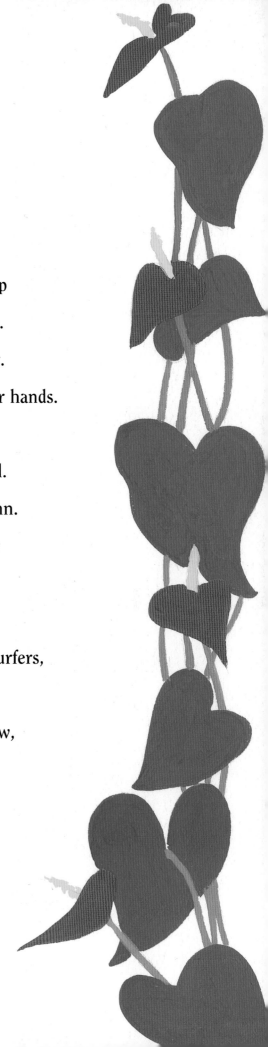

Each woman touched Keana's face,

and over the waves she seemed to fly.

Then she awoke in her own soft bed,

and the sun was rising in the sky.

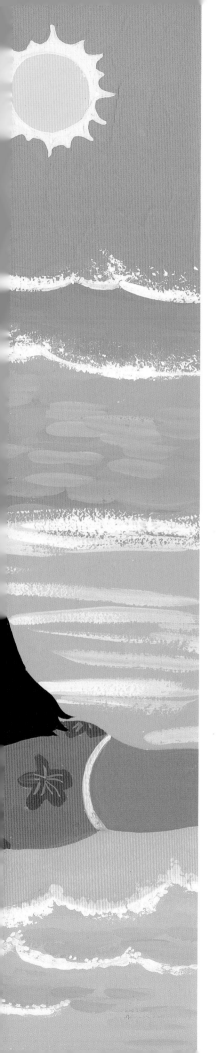

Keana jumped right out of bed.
Her day to surf was here at last.
"Come on, Uncle, let's catch a wave.
I may be new, but I'll learn fast."

Uncle took her to the beach.
He said, "Waves come in sets, you'll find.
Watch them, see them, really feel them,
understand them in your mind.

"It's a good day to learn," he said.
"The waves are gentle, but not too small.
Even so, you'll still wipe out—
that's what we call it when we fall.

"Just watch the waves, find the break,
and paddle out beyond the foam.
Pop up when the crest is best
to catch the wave and ride it home."

Keana tumbled off her board.

Time and time again she fell.

But she kept on, inspired by thoughts

of Māmala, Mary Ann, and Rell,

And all the surfers down through time—
man and woman, girl and boy.
She felt them lift her to her feet
and she popped up and stood with joy.

That day Keana learned to surf.
She rode the waves, but, even more,
she joined the surfing *'ohana*
that's touched all time and every shore.

So watch the waves, find the break,
paddle out beyond the foam,
and someday you may learn to surf.
Then you will ride that big wave home.

For Joe

Mahalos

Joe Eudovich
Dave Leonard
Hud Sturm

Design: Carol Colbath

Library of Congress Cataloging-in-publication Data

Golembe, Carla.
The story of surfing / Carla
Golembe ; illustrated by
Carla Golembe.
p.   cm.
Includes illustrations, glossary.
ISBN-10 1-57306-243-X
ISBN-13 978-1-57306-243-5
1. Surfing - Hawaii - Juvenile
fiction. 2. Hawaii - Juvenile fiction.
I. Title.
PZ7.G65 2006   [E]-dc21

Printed in Korea

CD recorded at Rendez-Vous Recording. Performer: Noelani K. Mahoe.

Carla Golembe is the author and illustrator of numerous books for children, including *The Story of Hula*,
which in 2004 won a Benjamin Franklin Award, presented by the Publishers Marketing Association.